PUFFIN BOOKS

GEORGE SPEAKS

For a long time, Laura has been wanting a little brother or sister to play with. But when George arrives, she's not so sure. He looks just like a little pig, with his round red face, squashy nose and tiny eyes all sunken in fat. But Laura soon discovers that George is no ordinary baby — in fact he's *extraordinary*, and everyone's life is turned upside down from the day George speaks!

A hilarious story from an ever-popular author.

Dick King-Smith was born near Bristol. After serving in the Grenadier Guards during the Second World War, he spent twenty years as a farmer in Gloucestershire, an experience which inspired many of his stories. He went on to teach at a village primary school. His first book, *The Fox Busters*, was published in 1978. Since then he has written a great number of children's books including *The Sheep-Pig* (winner of the *Guardian* Award), *Harry's Mad*, *Noah's Brother*, *The Hodgeheg*, *Martin's Mice*, *The Cuckoo Child* and many others. He is married, with three children and ten grandchildren, and lives in Avon.

D1143998

DICK KING-SMITH

George Speaks

ILLUSTRATED BY JUDY BROWN

PUFFIN BOOKS

PUFFIN BOOKS

Published by the Penguin Group
Penguin Books Ltd, 27 Wrights Lane, London W8 5TZ, England
Penguin Books USA Inc., 375 Hudson Street, New York, New York 10014, USA
Penguin Books Australia Ltd, Ringwood, Victoria, Australia
Penguin Books Canada Ltd, 10 Alcorn Avenue, Toronto, Ontario, Canada M4V 3B2
Penguin Books (NZ) Ltd, 182–190 Wairau Road, Auckland 10, New Zealand

Penguin Books Ltd, Registered Offices: Harmondsworth, Middlesex, England

First published by Viking Kestrel 1988
Published in Puffin Books 1989
10

Text copyright © Dick King-Smith, 1988
Illustrations copyright © Judy Brown, 1988
All rights reserved

Printed in England by Clays Ltd, St Ives plc
Filmset in Palatino

Chapter 1

Laura's baby brother George was four weeks old when it happened.

Laura, who was seven, had very much wanted a brother or sister for a long time. It would be so nice to have someone to play with, she thought. But when George was born, she wasn't so sure.

Everybody – her mother and father, the grandparents, uncles, aunts, friends – made such a fuss of him. And all of them

said how beautiful he was. Laura didn't
think he was. How could anyone with a
round red face and a squashy nose and little
tiny eyes all sunken in fat be called
beautiful? She looked at him as he lay
asleep in his carry-cot.

'Don't wake George up, will you?' her
mother had said. 'I'll be in the kitchen if you
want me.'

'I won't wake you,' Laura said to the
sleeping baby. 'And I don't want to sound
rude. But I must tell you something. You
look just like a little pig.'

And that was when it happened.

The baby opened his eyes and stared straight at her.

'Pig yourself,' he said.

Laura gasped. A shiver ran up her spine and her toes tingled.

'What did you say?' she whispered.

'I said, "Pig yourself",' said George. 'You're not deaf, are you?'

'No,' said Laura. 'No, it's just that I didn't expect you to say anything.'

'Why not?'

'Well, babies don't say proper words. They only make noises, like Goo-goo or Blur-blur or Wah.'

'Is that a fact?' said the baby.

'Yes,' said Laura. 'It is. However can you talk like that when you're only four weeks old? It's amazing! I must run and tell Mum.'

She turned to dash out of the room.

'Laura!' said the baby sharply.

Laura turned back.

'Yes, George?' she said.

The baby looked at her very severely, his forehead creased into a little frown.

'On no account are you to tell our mother,' he said. 'Or anyone else for that matter. This is a secret between you and me. Do you understand?'

'Yes, George,' said Laura.

'I've been waiting for some time now,' said George, 'to speak to you on your own. This is the first proper chance I've had, what with feeding and bathing and nappy-changing and people coming to see me all the time. And talk about making noises – that's all some of them do. They bend over me with silly grins on their faces, and then they come out with a load of rubbish. "Who's booful den?" "Who's a gorgeous Georgeous Porgeous?" "Diddums wassums Granny's ickle treasure?" It's an insult to the English language.'

'But George,' said Laura, 'how do you know the English language?'

'Well, I'm English, aren't I?'

'Yes, but how did you learn it?'

'Same way as you, I imagine. Listening to grown-ups talking. I wasn't born yesterday, you know.'

'But you're only four weeks old,' said Laura. 'How did you learn so quickly?'

'I'm a quick learner,' said George.

He waved his little arms and kicked his pudgy legs in the air.

'Talking's a piece of cake,' he said. 'Trouble is, I haven't learned to control my body very well yet. In fact, I'm afraid we'll have to postpone the rest of this conversation until another time.'

'Why?' asked Laura.

'I'm wet,' said George.

'Oh,' said Laura. 'Shall I go and tell Mummy you need changing?'

'Use your brains, Laura,' said George. 'You couldn't have known unless I'd told you, could you? You keep quiet. I'll tell her.'

'But you said it was going to be a secret between the two of us – you being able to talk, I mean.'

'So it is,' said George. 'I'll tell her in the way she expects. I've got her quite well trained,' and he shut his eyes and yelled

'Wah! Wah! Wah!' at the top of his voice.

His mother came in.

'What de matter with Mummy's lubbly lickle lambie?' she said.

She picked George up and felt him.

'Oh, he's soaking!' she said. 'No wonder he was crying, poor pettikins!'

She smiled at Laura as she changed the baby's nappy. 'It's the only way they can let

13

you know there's something wrong, isn't it?' she said.

'Yes, Mummy,' said Laura.

She caught George's eye as he lay across his mother's lap. It was no surprise to her that he winked.

Chapter 2

For the rest of that day Laura was in a state of great excitement. She kept grinning to herself and hugging herself and doing little dances when no one was looking.

Fancy having a baby brother who could talk! Think of all the things we can talk about, she thought. What a lot there will be for me to tell him! Or will there?

She watched George being bathed, kicking away just like any other small baby, while his mother supported his head with one hand and with the other flicked the

warm water over his sticking-out tummy.
I shouldn't be surprised, thought Laura,
if there's nothing I can tell him. He
probably knows it all already.

'He looks clever, doesn't he, Mum?' she
said.

'Clever?' said her mother, laughing.
'Why, he's only a baby, Laura. Babies don't
know anything. But he's booful, aren't you,
my little ookey-pookey poppet?'

'Gurgle-glug,' said George.

Laura didn't get a chance to be alone with George before bedtime. But she spent the whole night, it seemed, dreaming about him.

In one of these dreams she took him to school with her, and carried him into Assembly.

'Laura!' said the headmaster. 'That child is far too young to come to school.'

'But Sir,' said Laura, 'he's very intelligent.'

'Intelligent, is he?' said the headmaster,

while all the children laughed. 'I suppose he knows his tables?'

'Of course,' Laura said.

The headmaster leaned down towards the baby, who was sitting on Laura's lap. 'Well, young man,' he said, 'perhaps you could tell me the answer to this. What's three times nine?'

'Twenty-seven,' said George. He looked scornfully at the headmaster. 'I would have expected you to know that,' he said.

When Laura woke up next morning and remembered that dream, it seemed fantastic. Fantastic to think that a tiny baby could do sums! Or talk, for that matter. Was *that* all a dream – what she thought had

happened yesterday?
'I must make sure,'
she said, and she
jumped out of bed.
Peeping round the
door of George's room,

she saw that he was alone. Mummy was
downstairs getting breakfast and Daddy
was shaving in the bathroom. Laura went
in, closing the door behind her, and looked
into the cot.

'George!' she said softly. 'It's me, Laura.
Listen, George. What's three times nine?'

George smiled at her and waved his fat
little hands.

'Goo-goo,' he said. 'Goo-goo-goo.'

Laura's face crumpled. It *had* all been a
dream then! She burst into tears.

'Oh, come on, Laura,' said George testily.
'Don't be such a baby!'

'Oh George!' cried Laura, the tears running down her face. She bent over and kissed the top of his bald head.

'I thought . . .,' she said, 'I thought . . .'

'I know what you thought,' said George. 'Can't you take a joke? And do stop crying on me – it's bad enough being wet at the bottom end.'

'Sorry,' sniffed Laura.

'The answer to your question,' said George, 'is twenty-seven. Don't you know your tables?'

'Only two times and ten times,' said Laura.

George sighed. 'I can see you're going to need some help,' he said. 'Let's start with the three times table. Repeat after me,' and he began 'Three ones are three . . .'

They had just finished when the bedroom door suddenly opened and their father came in, rubbing his face with a towel.

'You're a funny old thing, aren't you?' he said to Laura.

'I don't know what you mean,' Laura said.

'Well, I was standing outside listening to you saying your tables, and you said everything twice over.'

'I remember it better that way,' Laura said.

'Blur-blur,' George said.

'Anyway you got them all right. I didn't know you knew your three times. Clever girl. Wonder if you'll be as clever when you're Laura's age, George?'

'Blur-blur-blur,' George said.

Downstairs, the telephone rang.

'It's for you,' their mother called, and their father went out of the room.

'Golly!' said Laura. 'We nearly gave the game away then! I didn't know Daddy had finished in the bathroom.'

George smiled.

'It was a close shave,' he said.

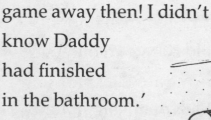

Chapter 3

There weren't all that many chances, Laura found, to talk to George. If there wasn't a grown-up with him, then he was likely to be asleep. He slept a great deal. Once, Laura had woken him from an afternoon nap and he had been quite grumpy.

'Don't you understand,' he had said, 'that I must have my eighteen hours?'

But sometimes it all worked out just right. Like the sunny Saturday morning when their mother had put George in his pram and said to Laura 'Would you like to push him round the garden for a little while?'

'At last we are alone,' said Laura in a dramatic voice, once they were as far as possible from the house.

'What's up?' said George. 'You sound worried.'

'I am,' said Laura. 'I need your advice.'

'Trouble with the three times table again?' said George.

'No, I know that. I was the only one in our class that did. My teacher at school was amazed.'

'So is your other teacher,' said George drily. 'Anyway, what's eating you?'

'It's the grown-ups,' Laura said. 'How are we going to stop them finding out about you? Daddy nearly did the other morning.'

She glanced towards the house. 'Suppose Mummy sees my lips moving now?' she said.

'So – you're talking to me,' said George. 'People do talk to babies. Endlessly. Sometimes they even wake them up to talk to them.'

'Yes, but babies don't talk back,' said Laura. 'Suppose someone came into a room and saw you talking?'

'That might be tricky,' said George. He wrinkled his little forehead in thought. Then he smiled.

'Got it!' he said. 'If that ever happens, you just pretend you're a ventriloquist.'

'A what?'

George sighed.

'A ventriloquist,' he said patiently, 'is someone who can throw his voice. He has a dummy on his lap, and he makes it seem as if the dummy is talking. I could be your dummy. You'd keep your lips quite still and

I'd say things like "A bottle of beer".'

'Why?' said Laura.

George sighed again.

'Forget it,' he said.

'But I can't forget it, George,' said Laura. 'This is what's worrying me. Here you are, only just born . . .'

'. . . six weeks today,' said George.

'. . . and yet you know your tables and long words like ven-whateveritwas and exactly how old you are. Other babies can't do any of those things. How can you?'

'To be honest with you, Laura,' said George in a serious voice, 'I don't know. All I can remember is looking around just after I arrived and finding everything very familiar. It was as though I'd seen it all before. There was a clock on the wall that said half past four, and I thought "Tea-time". And there was a calendar with the date on it – April the first – and I

thought "What a day to be born on." And a bit later on I heard Mummy and Daddy talking. "We must decide on a name," he

said. And she said, "Well, we agreed it's either Frederick or Charles, didn't we?" And I was just going to say, "Rubbish, I'm George", when one of them said, "What about George? It's a nice name," and the other said, "George! Yes, I like that." So I kept my mouth shut. Anyway, it would have been much too much of a shock for grown-ups. They don't have much imagination. But I couldn't resist letting you in on the secret.'

'But how much longer can we keep it secret?' asked Laura.

'Well,' said George, 'they're going to have to know sooner or later. I can't take too

much more of this Goo-goo-goo Blur-blur
Wah stuff – it gets pretty boring. But I plan
to take it gradually. Just the odd word to
begin with, the kind of thing they expect,
you know – "Baba" "Dada" "More" – that
sort of level.'

'You're going to say things like that quite
soon, you mean?' said Laura.

'That's right. Maybe it would be best to
start off by repeating words that they say to
me.'

'Like a parrot, you mean?'

'Yes,' said George. 'Then, once I get them
used to the idea that I'm an early developer,

I can speed things up a bit – feed them some simple sentences.'

'Like what?'

George wriggled uncomfortably. 'Like "George wants potty",' he said.

'Ssssh,' said Laura suddenly. 'Mummy's coming.'

'OK,' said George. 'There's no time like the present. Watch this.'

He waited until his mother's face appeared, looking down into the pram, and then he stared up at her and smiled.

'Mama!' said George loudly.

'Did you hear that, Laura?' she said in amazement. 'Did you hear what George just said?'

'Yes, Mummy,' said Laura.

'Only six weeks old and he says "Mama"! You heard him, didn't you?'

'Yes, Mummy.'

'You did say it, didn't you, baby?'

'Yes, Mummy,' said George.

Chapter 4

'George speaks!' cried the children's
mother, the moment their father came
home from work.

'What *do* you mean?'

'First of all he said "Mama".'

'Well, that's just a noise a baby makes.'

'Ah, but then he said "Yes, Mummy".
Didn't he, Laura? Laura had said to me

"Yes, Mummy", and George repeated it!'

'Like a parrot, you mean?'

'Yes.'

The children's father smiled. 'It hardly sounds likely,' he said drily.

He went into the bedroom and bent over the cot. 'Hullo, George,' he said to the baby and the baby replied 'Hullo, George.'

His father turned pale. 'I can't believe it's true,' he said.

'It's true,' said George.

'I don't think he can say a whole sentence yet, Daddy,' said Laura quickly. 'Just two words at a time. Shall I have a go now?'

She looked into the cot, trying hard not to giggle, and said, 'How many words can you say, George – only two?'

'Only two,' said George.

'You see?' said Laura to her parents.

'After all,' she said, 'he's not very old, is he?'

'I simply don't believe my ears,' said her father to her mother.

'Neither do I. What are we to do?'

Her father mopped his brow. 'I'm going to ring up the doctor,' he said, and they both went out of the room.

'Golly!' said Laura. 'What will you do now, George?'

'Take it easy, Laura,' said George.

Again he wrinkled his little forehead in thought.

'I think,' he said, 'that we're going to have to slow things down a bit. That's the trouble with grown-ups – something out of the ordinary happens and they panic. Children are so much more sensible.'

'But what will you say when the doctor comes?'

George waved a fat hand towards his mouth. 'Watch this space,' he said.

'Well now, young fellow,' said the doctor when he came, 'what's all this I hear?'

George stared blankly up at him.

'Only six weeks old and beginning to

talk? You'll be in *The Guinness Book of Records*!'

He turned to George's parents. 'He repeated the actual words after you, did you say?' he asked.

'Yes,' they said.

'Well well!' said the doctor in a jolly voice. 'Let's see if he'll do it for me!'

He bent down to George. 'Good evening,' he said, loudly and clearly.

George remained silent.

The doctor smiled. 'Perhaps he knows he shouldn't talk to strangers,' he said drily. 'You have a go.'

George's father cleared his throat nervously. 'Hullo, George,' he said.

'Goo-goo-goo,' said George.

'Speak to us, George,' said his father.

'Blur-blur-blur,' said George.

'I'm afraid I call that perfectly ordinary baby-talk,' said the doctor.

Laura grinned at her brother. 'Come on, George,' she said. 'Say something to the nice doctor.'

George smiled at his sister. Then he pursed up his little mouth and blew two loud, rude raspberries.

The doctor looked narrowly at the children's parents. 'Perhaps,' he said, 'you've been overdoing things. Take a break. Have a holiday. And next time this infant makes a funny noise, just say to yourselves quite calmly, "It is not possible for a baby to speak at the age of six weeks." Goodbye.'

Chapter 5

In the weeks that followed, George treated his parents with care. They were not ready, it was plain to him, to grasp just how different he was from other babies.

'No use expecting them to run before they can walk,' he said to Laura.

So he kept on, manfully, with his baby-

talk, but threw in the occasional couple of parrot-words as well, to reassure them.

They had agreed, after the doctor's visit, to keep George's gift a family secret. They did not know of the long conversations that George and Laura had when alone.

George made use of these talks to improve his lot. Speech and knowledge

were his, but bodily control was not. For that he would have to wait but not as long, he determined, as an ordinary baby. He planned to improve matters, with Laura's help.

The first way was to use her as book-holder and page-turner, for reading, George was sure, would help to pass the long boring hours of babyhood. They had to be careful, in case someone came in, and Laura always had a big picture-book ready, to put over the top of whatever story George was reading to her.

The second improvement which George arranged was in the matter of food. 'Milk, milk and more milk,' he said to Laura. 'I'm fed up with the stuff. Next time we go down to the supermarket with Mummy, have a good look at the tinned baby-foods. They're on a high shelf and I can't read the labels from my pram. See what varieties they've got. I'd give my eye-teeth for a change from milk. If I had any.'

So the next time they went shopping,
Laura took a tin off the shelf and popped it
into the trolley when her mother wasn't
looking.

'What's this?' said her
mother when they
reached the check-out.
'Baby-food? Minced
Beef and Vegetables?'

'It's for George,' Laura said.

'But he's barely two months old, Laura. It's far too early to feed him solids. Put it back where you found it.'

'But Mummy,' said Laura, 'I'm sure he'll eat it.'

'Eat it,' said George from the depths of the pram.

The check-out lady stared. 'D'you know,' she said, 'just for a second I thought that that baby said something!'

'Blur-blur-blur,' said George, and thankfully and hastily his mother put the tin of baby-food down with the rest of her shopping, paid, and hurried out.

'There's no way that a baby of George's
age is going to eat this stuff, Laura,' she
said when they got home. She tipped the
minced beef and vegetables into a bowl.

'He'll simply spit it out,' she said.

She dipped a spoon into the bowl and
held it to George's mouth. 'He's just too
young to think that it's nice,' she said.

George golloped the spoonful down.

'It's nice,' he said.

After that, it was easy. George made a simple plan.

'I'll choose the menu,' he said to Laura, 'and tell you my choices. Then you say them to me and I just repeat them.'

So at feeding-times Laura would say, in front of her mother, 'What would you like, George? Bacon Casserole?' and George would say, 'Bacon Casserole.'

'And for afters? Peach Melba?'

'Peach Melba.'

Or it might be 'Chicken and Mushroom?' and 'Fruit Delight?'

'Chicken and Mushroom' and 'Fruit Delight.'

Sometimes, of course, Laura was at school, and then George just had to hope for the best. If he was very lucky, it might be his favourite mixture – Chocolate Pudding on top of Lamb Hot-Pot. Taking pot luck, he called it.

*

The third improvement that George
wanted was to do with quite a different
sort of pot.

'Laura,' he said, 'can you remember what
it was like when you were in nappies?'

'No.'

'Lucky you,' said George. 'I can tell you
that it is most unpleasant. Potty-training –
training Mummy and Daddy to it, I mean –
must begin as soon as possible.'

'But how will you balance, George?'

'Someone will have to hold me, that's obvious. But they'll be only too glad to, if they can dispense with nappies. I just want you to help me break them in to the idea – in the usual way – and then they'll be able to manage on their own.'

In fact, his mother's training began that very day. George winked at Laura, and Laura said, 'Mummy, d'you

think George would go on a pot?'

'A pot,' said George.

'Don't be silly, Laura,' said her mother. 'He's too small.'

'A pot!' shouted George in a loud commanding voice.

Dazedly, his mother put him on it, and he went.

Chapter 6

Ordinary babies grizzle or yell when they are uncomfortable or hungry. George made sure, from now on, that his needs were met. He did it, quite simply, not by asking but by giving orders.

At any time of day or night, the cry 'A  pot! A pot!' was heard, and someone rushed to do his bidding. Also he did not wait long before beginning to order his own meals direct.

To do all this meant further training for his parents. First, George dropped the

parrot-fashion trick of repeating what
was said to him. To be sure, when his
mother said 'Good morning' he replied
with those same two words, but then

we all do that. However, when, as was her
habit, his mother said, 'Who's a good boy!'
(because the baby always answered 'Good
boy!' which made her go weak at the knees)
George now replied, 'I am, of course.'

'Oh!' cried his mother in delight, 'what a clever little ookey-pookey bunny wabbit!'

'Cut that out!' said George sternly. 'And I

want muesli and banana for breakfast.'

From that moment, neither George's mother (from shock) nor George (with relief) ever spoke baby-talk again.

But it was still only to Laura that George revealed his full powers of speech and reason. To his parents he now spoke the occasional short sentence, almost always beginning, 'I want . . .' In front of other relations, his grandparents for example, he usually kept silent, either pretending to be asleep or perhaps favouring them with a gracious smile.

'Aren't you a beautiful boy!' they might say, and George would reply, 'Yes.'

'George speaks!' they cried to one another, but George had no intention, yet, of showing them how much.

'I think my first birthday will be the right time,' he said to Laura.

'Right time for what?'

'My maiden speech in the house.'

'I don't understand,' said Laura.

George looked at her in a kindly way.

'It's difficult for you, I know,' he said. 'But the time is coming when I shall feel the need of adult conversation. Not that I don't enjoy talking to you, Laura – don't think that for a moment – but there are a lot of things that you don't know much about . . . politics, history, religion, the arts. Take

58

writing, for instance. I'm beginning to get the hang of holding a pencil but at present it won't make the marks I want it to. So I can't put my ideas down on paper yet. That will come. But in the meantime I'm getting very tired of limiting my gift of speech. So – on my first birthday – I'm going to hoist my flag to the mast-head and show myself in my true colours.'

'I don't know what all that means,' said Laura.

'You will do, dear,' said George. 'When you're a little older.'

In one way especially, George was exactly like every other normal healthy baby. He loved his grub. As long as food was put in front of him, George would eat it.

He differed, however, from other babies in being extremely choosy and, of course, in having the power to make his preferences known.

Not surprisingly then, George had ordered the food for all the meals on his birthday, and had done so well in advance.

'My handwriting leaves a certain amount to be desired at present,' he had said to his mother some days earlier. 'So if you will be good enough to fetch paper and pencil, I will dictate the menus to you.'

'Yes, George,' said his mother, and did as she was told.

'Now then,' said George. 'Let us begin at the beginning. Breakfast. It is most important to have a good lining to the stomach at the start of the day. It sets you up for the rest of it, don't you agree, Mummy?'

'Yes, George,' his mother said.

'Right then,' said George. 'I've been thinking about this during our recent visits to the supermarket. For instance, there is a brand of tinned creamed rice called Ambrosia. You know the meaning of that word, I presume?'

His mother shook her head. George sighed.

'It means "food fit for a god". Rather suitable, don't you think?'

'Yes, George.'

'I'll start with a tin of that. And I should like it well laced with Golden Syrup.'

'Yes, George.'

'I have a sweet tooth, you see,'
said George. 'In fact . . .'
and he explored the
inside of his mouth
with a fat finger,' . . .

in fact, I have ten sweet teeth.'

George's mother smiled proudly.

'Is that all you want for breakfast?' she
said.

'Oh goodness me, no, Mummy,' said
George a trifle sharply. 'We're talking about
meals for my birthday, remember? Special

meals, not just the ordinary old humdrum food.'

'Yes, George. What next then?'

'Eggs,' said George. 'Large, brown, free-range eggs. Scrambled. Quite the most civilized way to eat eggs, in my opinion.'

'On toast?'

'If it's done properly,' said George. 'Not the way you and Daddy usually have it – left to get cold when it comes out of the toaster and then just a scrape of margarine on it. I want my toast spread while it's hot so that the butter sinks into it. Plenty of butter too. West Country Green Pastures is a good brand. And I shall need something to wash it all down with.'

'Orange juice?'

'If you mean that stuff that comes out of cartons – no. Squeeze some fresh oranges, please – smallish ones for choice, they're  sweeter – and add a teaspoonful of demerara sugar. Now then, about lunch.'

Lunch was to be easier for the cook, since George wanted his favourite Lamb Hot-Pot,  with Chocolate Pudding for afters, but his instructions for the birthday tea were more demanding.

There was to be jelly ('strawberry,' said George), and ice-cream ('Neapolitan'), and banana custard and tinned peaches and Swiss Roll; and, of course, the birthday cake.

'I'll leave the actual ingredients to you, Mummy,' said George graciously, 'but please be generous with the marzipan and icing-sugar, and I'd like some of those pink roses on top. And don't forget the candle.'

'Of course I won't,' said his baffled mother. One candle, she thought. Can it be true that he is only going to be one year old?

'Will that be all, George?' she said.

'Oh, I think so,' said George. 'It's rather modest, I know, but then quality is more important than quantity, don't you think?'

Afterwards he told Laura what he had ordered.

'I must keep my strength up, you see,' he said. 'It's going to be a busy day. I shall have a lot on my plate.'

'You certainly will,' said Laura.

Chapter 7

Soon it was the last day of March, the last
day of the first year of George's life. During
the previous three months he had revealed
much more to his mother and father. He
spoke to them at greater and greater
length, and, when he judged them ready,
disclosed that he could read. So well trained
had they become that when they said,
'What would you like for a birthday present?'
and he replied, 'An encyclopaedia,'
they did not even flinch. Now everything
was ready for the birthday party the
next day.

'George,' his mother had said, 'would
you like me to ask some other bab . . .
children?'

'Certainly not,' George had said. 'This party is for grown-ups, except of course for Laura. Grandparents, uncles, aunts – that sort of thing. I shall want to say a few words

to them. They can have a slice of cake, and no doubt they will expect endless cups of tea.'

'What would you like to drink, George?'

'Anything except milk.'

*

'Just think,' said Laura that evening when she came to say good-night to George. He was in his bedroom, practising walking, something he had only lately learned. 'Just think, George – in the morning you'll be a whole year old!'

'I shall feel my age,' said George. 'It's been a long time. But things should

improve now that I've found my feet. By the way, did you get me the present that I asked for?'

'Yes,' said Laura. 'A notepad and some felt pens, like you said. Though I should have thought you'd have liked a surprise.'

'I shall get enough surprises tomorrow from the relations, you'll find,' said George somewhat sourly. 'Rattles, cuddly toys, books with big pictures of c-a-t-s and d-o-g-s. At least your present will soon be very useful to me.'

*

Laura lay awake a long time that night, thinking about her baby brother. Not that you can call him a baby, she thought. Or ever could, really. I mean, he looks like one, but there's never been a baby as clever as George is. How much he had helped her! No one else in her class knew all their tables right up to twelve times, like she did. No one else could add and subtract and share

like she could. And certainly no one was as good at General Knowledge. Why, she knew how many legs a spider had and what was the capital of France and who wrote *The Jungle Book* and who won the Battle of Hastings and dozens of other things – all because George had told her.

She remembered the dream she had had when he was very small. Golly, wouldn't the headmaster be amazed at George now!

When she woke next morning she couldn't
think, just for a second, why she felt

excited. Then it came to her. It was the First
of April! It was George's birthday! At that
moment she heard her mother's voice,
calling her urgently. Laura put on her
dressing-gown and ran, to find both her
parents bending over George's cot.

'What's the matter?' she said.

'George doesn't look well,' said her mother in a worried voice.

'He won't speak,' said her father. 'We've called him and called him, but he doesn't answer.'

Laura looked into the cot. George was lying quite still with his eyes shut. He was blowing very quickly and noisily through his mouth. Then, suddenly, he seemed to stop breathing, and his mouth closed, and his face began to go red.

'Oh George!' cried Laura. 'Whatever's the

matter? Speak to me, George, please! Say something!'

All at once George opened his eyes and his mouth and let out the breath that he had been holding and burst out laughing.

'D'you know what you lot are?' he said at last.

'What?' they said.

'April Fools!' said George happily.

Chapter 8

George swallowed the last mouthful of
scrambled egg and gave a loud burp. He
smiled at his sister.

'Do you remember, Laura,' he said,
'when you used to hold me over your
shoulder and pat me on the back to bring
up my wind?'

Laura nodded.

'So much pleasanter,' said George, 'when one can do these things for oneself.'

'Have you had enough to eat, George?' said his mother.

'Thank you, yes. An excellent breakfast, Mummy,' said George. 'You are to be congratulated.'

He turned in his high-chair. 'Daddy,' he said, 'could I borrow your daily newspaper for a moment?'

'Of course you can,' said his dazed
father. Reading the paper, he thought, on
his first birthday.

'Come to think of it,' said George, 'it
would be simpler if you could find the place
for me and read it out. I find newspapers
difficult to handle.'

'Which bit d'you want, George?'

'My horoscope,' said George. 'The section is called THIS IS YOUR DAY, round about page twenty-five. I'm Aries.'

'Aries,' said his father. 'Let's see. It says, "You're under a lot of pressure today."'

George burped again. 'That's true,' he said.

'But you carry more weight than you realize.'

George looked down at his stomach. 'Possibly,' he said.

'And you will have everyone falling over themselves to make it a pleasant day for you.'

'Splendid!' said George. 'Now, there should be a special item entitled IF IT'S YOUR BIRTHDAY.'

'Oh yes, here we are. It says, "You will grow in stature in the coming year."'

George nodded.

'You will take great strides forward.'

George nodded again.

'Your knowledge, wit and wisdom will be the admiration of all.'

'Remarkable,' said George. 'The fellow has me to a T.'

For the rest of the morning George practised writing with his new felt pens, and read his new encyclopaedia, Laura turning the pages for him.

Then, after his favourite lunch, he had a good rest, to be ready for his birthday party. He went to bed and slept like a baby.

At George's birthday party, everything was ready. All the guests had arrived; the four grandparents and an assortment of uncles and aunts, including a large jolly uncle newly home from abroad, who had never met George. They had handed over their gifts, and now sat round the loaded table.

'Come on, everyone!' said the large jolly uncle. 'Let's sing Happy Birthday!'

'Excuse me,' said Laura quickly. 'George doesn't want the singing yet. He wants to eat first, and then, after he's cut the cake, you can sing.'

'Well, well!' laughed the large jolly uncle. 'And then what happens?'

'Then,' said Laura, 'George speaks.'

So they all ate, and then George cut the

cake, with Laura's help, and after that everyone sang, 'Happy Birthday, dear George, Happy Birthday to you.'

'Speech!' shouted the large jolly uncle, winking at the others.

Then Laura wiped a mixture of ice-cream and cake off George's face and took off his plastic bib, and George rapped with a spoon on the tray of his high-chair, and all fell silent.

'Ladies and gentlemen,' said George.
'I am delighted to welcome you all here
today, and I trust you will forgive me if I
remain seated. Standing up in a high-chair
is, you will agree, a dangerous business.'

He paused and looked round at the circle
of astonished faces. The large jolly uncle
gaped.

'First,' George went on, 'I should like to thank you all for the gifts which you have brought. I am sure you meant well.

'Next, I wish to thank my parents for the excellent meal which they have so kindly provided.

'And thirdly, I want to take this opportunity to say how grateful I am to my sister Laura.'

Laura blushed.

'Without her understanding, support and affection,' George continued, 'this past year would indeed have been a trying time for me.'

He paused to take a sip of orange juice from his feeding-cup.

'For a long time now,' he said, 'Laura has
known of my personal good fortune,
namely the possession of intelligence
beyond my years. Or rather, I should have
said, beyond my *year*. Ha ha.'

'Ha ha,' said several voices nervously.

'More recently,' said George, 'my parents
have also become aware that I am not, shall
we say, as other babies are, but to the rest of
you it may have come as something of a
shock. May I say I hope the shock is not

an unpleasant one. All of you are of course much older than myself, some' (and he nodded politely towards the four grandparents) 'very much older. You therefore have what I lack, namely experience of the world, and I look forward to many interesting discussions with you all on a variety of subjects. And now, if you will forgive me, I must leave you. Sleep is important at my age, and it has been a tiring day.'

George bent forward in his chair in a kind of bow.

'Once again,' he said, 'thank you all for coming.'

Laura looked round at the faces of the others. Her parents were smiling proudly. The grandparents, uncles and aunts sat bemused, scratching their heads or shaking them in disbelief, their eyes wide, their

eyebrows raised. The large jolly uncle looked as though he had been hit with a sledge-hammer.

'Laura,' said George. 'Perhaps you would assist me down from this high-chair.'

How little he is, thought Laura, and how helpless still in many ways, yet how clever to make such a speech. She raised her hands and began to clap, and her mother and father joined in, and soon everyone was clapping. Then Laura lifted George down, and held his hand as he walked, not too steadily but with great dignity, out of the room.

'Thanks, Laura,' said George later when she had tucked him up in bed. 'And thanks again for the felt pens. I tried them out this morning. The pad is over there on the table. Have a look.'

Laura picked up the notepad that she had given him and there, in big red capitals, were the words:

GEORGE SPEAKS

'Golly, that's good, George,' she said. 'And what a speech it was! Why, when you grow up, you could be anything you wanted! You could make speeches like that in Parliament – you could be the Prime Minister!'

'That wouldn't get my vote,' said George.

'Well, you could be a Judge.'

'The verdict is "No".'

'A Brain Surgeon then.'

'Not on your life.'

'An explorer.'

'No way.'

Laura racked her brains to think of someone really important. There was the Queen of course, but then she didn't see how George could become a King. 'I know!' she said. 'You could be the Archbishop of Canterbury!'

'For Heaven's sake,' said George, 'I don't want to be any of those things. I want to do something that's fun.'

'Like what?' Laura said.

George yawned.

'I'll tell you a secret, Laura,' he said.

'When I grow up, I'm going to write funny stories for children.'

And d'you know, when George grew up, that's exactly what he did do. Would you believe it!